TECH LIVING

HIGH-TECH EVERYDAY SCIENCE

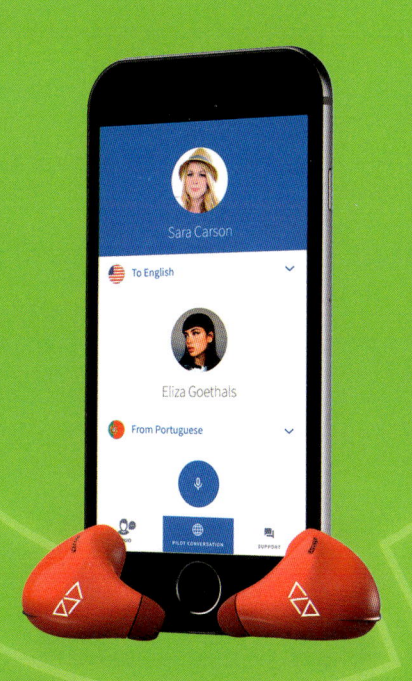

KELLY SPENCE

CRABTREE Publishing Company
www.crabtreebooks.com

TECHNO PLANET

Author: Kelly Spence

Editors: Sarah Eason, John Andrews, and Petrice Custance

Proofreader and indexer: Wendy Scavuzzo

Editorial director: Kathy Middleton

Design: Paul Myerscough, Paul Oakley, and Jane McKenna

Cover design: Paul Myerscough

Photo research: Rachel Blount

Production coordinator and Prepress technician: Margaret Amy Salter

Print coordinator: Margaret Amy Salter

Consultant: David Hawksett

Produced for Crabtree Publishing Company by Calcium Creative.

Photo Credits:

t=Top, tr=Top Right, tl=Top Left, b=Bottom, br=Bottom Right, bl=Bottom Left, bc=Bottom Center

Autism2Ability, Inc.: (Photograph provided courtesy of Autism2Ability. App2Talk & Autism2Ability are trademarks owned by Autism2Ability, Inc. and used herein with permission) 20; CuteCircuit: Theodoros Chliapas 18–19; Lightform, Inc.: 22b; Perfect Company: 10; Petcube, Inc./petcube.com: 14–15; Sensorwake: 9; Shutterstock: Chesky 11b, Chombosan 3, 5, 12b, Davorana 28br, Mike Flippo 28t, Halfpoint 22–23, Hurst Photo 29bl, Alexander Kirch 7, Daniel Krason 11t, Ktsdesign 27, Lucky Business 14tr, Maxbelchenko 12–13, Panatphong 29br, Marina Pousheva 25, Quality Stock Arts 6, Sdecoret 4, Ned Snowman 29tl, Speedimaging 29tr, Wk1003mike26; Sleep Number: 8; Snap Inc.: 18; Starship Technologies: 17; Waverly Labs: 1, 21; Wikimedia Commons: 28bc, Chrissshe 24, Alexander Klink 16.

Cover: Shutterstock: Mark Nazh

Library and Archives Canada Cataloguing in Publication

Spence, Kelly, author
    Tech living / Kelly Spence.

(Techno planet)
Includes index.
Issued in print and electronic formats.
ISBN 978-0-7787-3605-9 (hardcover).--
ISBN 978-0-7787-3619-6 (softcover).--
ISBN 978-1-4271-1993-3 (HTML)

      1. Technological innovations--Social aspects--Juvenile literature.
2. Technological innovations--Juvenile literature. 3. Technology--Social aspects--Juvenile literature. 4. Technology--Juvenile literature. I. Title.

T173.8.S666 2017   j303.48'3   C2017-903603-3
                                             C2017-903604-1

Library of Congress Cataloging-in-Publication Data

CIP available at the Library of Congress

Crabtree Publishing Company
www.crabtreebooks.com   1-800-387-7650

Printed in Canada/092017/PB20170719

Copyright © **2018 CRABTREE PUBLISHING COMPANY**. All rights reserved. No part of this publication may be reproduced, stored in a retrieval system or be transmitted in any form or by any means, electronic, mechanical, photocopying, recording, or otherwise, without the prior written permission of Crabtree Publishing Company. In Canada: We acknowledge the financial support of the Government of Canada through the Canada Book Fund for our publishing activities.

Published in Canada
Crabtree Publishing
616 Welland Ave.
St. Catharines, Ontario
L2M 5V6

Published in the United States
Crabtree Publishing
PMB 59051
350 Fifth Avenue, 59th Floor
New York, New York 10118

Published in the United Kingdom
Crabtree Publishing
Maritime House
Basin Road North, Hove
BN41 1WR

Published in Australia
Crabtree Publishing
3 Charles Street
Coburg North
VIC, 3058

CONTENTS

Tech at Home	4
A Smart Abode	6
Sweet Dreams!	8
Smart Kitchen	10
High-tech Garage	12
Pet Tech	14
Smart Home Shopping	16
Smart Wear	18
Cutting-edge Communication	20
Electronic Entertainment	22
Brainwaves	24
Future Fantastic	26
Tech Timeline	28
Glossary	30
Learning More	31
Index and About the Author	32

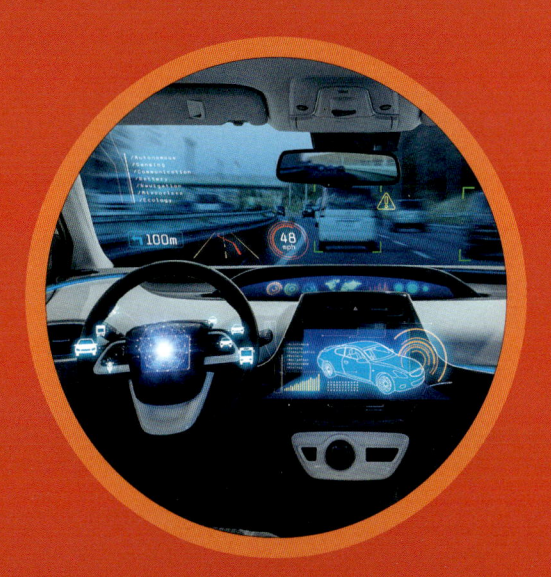

TECH AT HOME

Technology in the 21st century touches every part of our lives. It reaches everywhere, including the four walls we call home. "The Internet of Things" (IoT) is a phrase used to describe the billions of smart devices that send and receive information through the Internet. It is estimated that by the year 2020, about 200 billion smart devices will be connected to the Internet—about 26 for each person on the planet! Many of these devices will be in our homes.

WIRELESS CONNECTIVITY

From opening doors to boiling a kettle from bed, smartphone technology is making our lives easier in surprising ways. As new technologies are developed, the wireless **networks** that connect smart devices become more powerful and more reliable. Mobile networks are referred to by generation, which is represented by the letter "G." The first generation, or 1G, used **analog** technology. We now use 4G **digital** technology, which is able to process more information than 3G. By around 2022, an even more powerful 5G will begin to replace 4G.

Smart technology has already transformed the way that we communicate, work, and shop. Soon it will transform our homes, too.

MAKING CONNECTIONS

There are different ways to access cellular networks. While some devices require a plug to work, many more operate using wireless technology. Two common systems used to wirelessly transmit data are **Wi-Fi** and **Bluetooth**. Wi-Fi is short for "wireless fidelity." Places where Wi-Fi is available are called **hotspots**. Bluetooth is used to connect devices over short distances. It does not need access to the Internet. For example, music in our homes can be sent from a smartphone to a wireless speaker via Bluetooth.

ENDLESS POSSIBILITIES

Homes are going high-tech. Need to turn up the heat or close the window shades? Talk to the app on a smartphone. Bored? Xbox or PlayStation are there. Worried your parents are going to say you are eating too fast and that you are going to get sick? HAPIfork vibrates and flashes to warn you to slow down. No matter what you want to do at home, there is or may soon be an app or smart device for that!

*How do you listen to your favorite tunes? The cutting-edge technology you use today could soon become out-of-date as smart tech devices become even more **innovative**.*

A SMART ABODE

An abode is a home. Homes are smart these days. Computer-controlled gadgets are often called "smart" because they are able to perform tasks that appear intelligent. Smart homes are living spaces that are wired with new technologies that make them more **efficient**, comfortable, and secure. They are often controlled by a control center, such as the Amazon Echo. This voice-activated device **syncs** with other devices that control other electronic systems, such as the **thermostat**, lights, and entertainment systems.

COMMAND CENTER

Smart speakers act as the control center in many smart homes. The Amazon Echo "wakes up" when the word "Alexa" is spoken, which is the name given to the device's software. The Echo records the voice command, then sends it through the Internet to a cloud-based program. Software **converts** the information into a command and sends it to the appropriate website, such as a music-streaming site. Alexa can learn new commands, called skills, by connecting extra electronics and software to the system. Designers have also given Alexa a sense of humor. She can crack jokes, such as "What's a zombie's favorite vacation destination?" (Answer: The Dead Sea!) These bonus features are known as "Easter eggs."

How about asking a robot to vacuum your home?! Smart vacuums travel around the home independently, cleaning up dirt as they move.

TECHNO PLANET

The Roomba is the world's most popular robotic vacuum. This **autonomous** device uses technology to **navigate**. The robot is equipped with **sensors**, which gather information about its surroundings. An onboard computer processes the information, and this keeps the robot from bumping into walls or driving off a staircase. When its battery runs low, the Roomba drives back to its **dock** to charge. This same technology has been used to design devices that mop floors and clean pools, too.

HOME SECURITY

There are also dozens of smart home-security systems that provide surveillance 24 hours a day, seven days a week. Video cameras stream live surveillance video to your smartphone or tablet. A smartphone can use an app to send a wireless signal to a smart lock to open it, like a key. Once the key signal is recognized by the lock, the mechanical parts inside the lock open.

Soon people will be able to keep their homes secure and monitor any activity happening there just by checking their smartphones.

SWEET DREAMS!

Experts, such as the Centers for Disease Control and Prevention (CDC) in the United States, recommend that adults get at least seven hours of sleep each night. A 2014 study by the CDC reported that one in three adults was not getting enough rest. Today, technology is being used to monitor and help people get a good night's sleep.

POWERING DOWN

Smartphones give off a bright blue light that helps people see the screen on sunny days. At night, the blue light from electronic devices interferes with the body's ability to produce melatonin—a hormone that helps a person fall asleep. The blue light tricks your mind into thinking it is still daytime. The f.lux app fixes this on a smartphone or computer. Users enter in their geographical location, then the app figures out the time of sunrise and sunset based on that information. As the sun sets and natural light fades, the screen gradually turns warmer colors, such as red and orange. This results in less stimulation for the brain. Apple has developed a similar program for the iPhone, called Night Watch.

SLEEP SMART

The Sleep Number 360 is a smart bed that has built-in technology to help people sleep well. Sensors inside the bed detect movement. Air pockets inflate to raise or lower the mattress as a person tosses and turns. If a person is snoring, the bed will raise their head. The bed is connected to an app that tracks heartbeat, breathing, and movements. The app can also send a person an alert that advises them when to go to bed to get the proper amount of rest.

Getting a good night's sleep will become much easier as more people invest in a smart bed such as the Sleep Number 360.

RISE AND SHINE

Companies are always looking for inventive ways to help people wake up. The Sensorwake alarm clock uses a new twist to get people out of bed. Instead of sound or light, it uses smells. People can choose from scents such as toast, coffee, or chocolate. Before going to bed, a capsule is loaded into the clock. When the alarm goes off, the chosen scent is released for two minutes. After three minutes, an alarm goes off to wake people who might still be snoozing!

You could soon be waking up to the scent of your favorite food or drink rather than the buzz of an alarm clock.

SMART KITCHEN

Toasters, kettles, and microwaves. For a long time, technology has been used to make life easier in the kitchen. Now, from how we grocery shop to how we cook, amazing new tech is finding its way into the modern kitchen.

GET CONNECTED

A fridge that speaks to the Internet—how cool! The LG InstaView refrigerator has a large **touch screen** on its door. Users can order groceries and even send messages to other family members. Tap the touch screen twice and it turns clear, showing you what is inside the fridge. At the store and forgot to see if you are out of eggs or orange juice? No worries—just connect your smartphone to the Internet-connected cameras inside this smart fridge to check.

There are also smart ovens that let users control and monitor the oven remotely via a smartphone. You can choose a recipe from the oven's recipe bank and it will preheat to the correct temperature. In the future, a smart fridge might even be able to roast a chicken in its own oven compartment.

SMALL, BUT MIGHTY SMART

Smart electric cooking pots are tiny time-savers. Using a smartphone, users can check on the temperature, set the cooking time, and change settings to warm or even turn off the cooking pot.

Perfect Bake Pro is an app-connected scale. The app has a variety of recipes to follow. The scale shows the weight of flour or whatever ingredient you are adding to the mixing bowl. It guides you to make sure you add only what is needed, when it is needed. The app also makes sure that you mix and bake for the correct amount of time.

Cooking and baking will become smarter and easier with scales such as the Perfect Bake Pro. This supersmart scale is linked to an app that tells you the exact amount of each ingredient needed to make the perfect dish.

Wireless tech means you can control all your kitchen devices from a smartphone or tablet.

Smart fridges make grocery shopping easy—simply check the fridge contents on your smartphone when at a food store and buy what you need.

TECHNO PLANET

Not fond of the family's favorite casserole? Trick yourself into enjoying it! Project Nourished uses **virtual reality (VR)** to deliver a whole new dining experience. Virtual reality tricks a person's senses. Diners put on a headset that simulates an eating environment, such as a sushi restaurant in Japan. An **atomizer** sprays the scent of the food into the air. An eating utensil with built-in sensors shows the hand moving in the virtual world. A special device is attached to the jaw and transmits chewing sounds to the ear. Project Nourished was inspired by a scene in the movie Hook, when Peter Pan uses his imagination to change bowls of goop into a delicious meal!

11

HIGH-TECH GARAGE

In a few years, your home garage may look quite different. Check out the self-driving car. It is equipped with cutting-edge technology that allows the vehicle to operate without a driver behind the wheel. Passengers can sit back and relax as the car's different systems provide a safe and smooth ride.

ARE WE THERE YET?

Self-driving cars require **global positioning system (GPS)** software to plot a journey from one destination to another. Different sensors monitor the surroundings of the car as it travels. Cameras act like the car's eyes by reading signs and road markings. Sensors are mounted on different parts of the vehicle to detect nearby obstacles. A central computer analyzes all the information gathered by a car's different systems. That computer then controls the vehicle's brakes, speed, and steering. Companies such as Google, Uber, and BMW are working on versions of the self-driving car. Some people are concerned about their safety, but it is only a matter of time before we see these cars in our garages.

TECH TOYS

Leaning up against the wall of your garage is the e-bike—perfect for going the distance. Electric bicycles give riders the option of relying on power to move, or to pedal as though on a regular bicycle. Over in the corner is the hoverboard. A throwback to Marty McFly's ride in *Back to the Future II*, today's hoverboards do not actually hover above the ground. They work like powered skateboards. A **gyroscope** adjusts the tilt of the board to maintain balance. A computerized motor sends power to the wheels. Stand between the wheels and ride off—with a little practice!

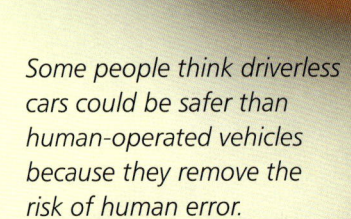

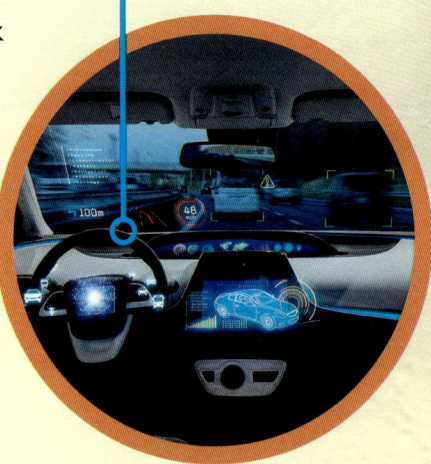

Some people think driverless cars could be safer than human-operated vehicles because they remove the risk of human error.

12

Hoverboarding to school, college, and even work might become a cool and common form of transportation!

TECHNO PLANET

Step aside Segway—it might be time to add a WalkCar to the collection of personal travel toys. Simply step on this flat, laptop-sized gizmo, lean forward, and off you go. WalkCar can reach speeds of up to 6.2 miles per hour (10 kph) and can travel more than 7 miles (11 km) before needing a recharge. WalkCars are small enough to fit into a backpack.

PET TECH

In the United States and Canada, more than 40% of all households have at least one pet dog, and at least 35% of all households have a pet cat. We love our pets! We also love technology. Put the two together and you get some amazing pet gadgets.

HIGH-TECH KIBBLE

Not sure how much food to put in your best friend's bowl? SmartBowl tells pet owners when they have poured exactly the right amount of food for their cat or dog. Smart feeders automatically release food for a pet. These feeders can be set for a particular time and amount of food. A smartphone app confirms that your pet has been fed and tells you how much food is left.

PET-ERTAINMENT

Entertaining pets and checking in on them can be difficult while you are at school and your parents are at work. Petcube is a camera that lets pet owners with a smartphone check in on their pets. The owner can even play with their pet remotely by using a built-in laser toy. PetChatz not only has a camera, but also dispenses treats when your pet performs tricks or shows good behavior. A special ringtone lets your pet know you are calling. PetChatz then rewards Fido or Fluffy with a treat for coming into view.

iFetch is a device that shoots a ball out whenever the ball is dropped into the attached funnel. Dogs can be trained to retrieve a ball and drop it into the device. The Passport Pet Access Smart Door is a pet door with an electronic key that attaches to your pet's collar. When the key comes close, the door opens. This lets your pet go in and out whenever it wants, but stops other animals from doing the same.

*This vet is scanning a **microchip** that is under a cat's skin. Microchipping allows owners to keep track of their furry friends.*

LOST AND FOUND

Keeping your dog in a yard without a tall fence can be a challenge. Invisible fences are electronic versions of a traditional fence. A buried cable sends a signal to your dog's collar, telling your pet that this is the boundary. But what happens if your best friend escapes from home? A vet can put a microchip under a pet's skin. If a pet gets lost, animal shelters can scan the chip and contact the registered owner. There are also many types of GPS-enabled pet tracking devices. Attach one to your pet's collar and you can track it wherever it goes.

The secret life of your dog or cat might not be a secret for much longer! The Petcube will film their antics while you are away from home.

SMART HOME SHOPPING

It is becoming less and less necessary to go to stores to buy groceries, clothes, and many other items. Build a list and shop online—technology makes it easy to do.

TALKING TRASH

Build a shopping list as you toss out the garbage or recycling. GeniCan is a smartphone app with a barcode reader. Simply swipe the reader over the barcode on an empty bag of rice or jar of peanut butter. The item will be added to a list on the GeniCan app on your phone. No barcode? No problem. Hold the item in front of the scanner for a few seconds and GeniCan will ask what you would like to add to the list. Simply tell it what you are holding before you toss it in the can. One day soon, GeniCan will automatically connect to online ordering.

LIST TO PURCHASE

Hiku is more than a chunky fridge magnet. Scan a barcode or tell the device which groceries you need and it creates a shopping list on your smartphone. Planned updates will add online price comparisons and complete online ordering.

Dash Buttons from Amazon are little electronic Wi-Fi devices that can be programmed to order anything from paper towels to dish soap. Tap a button and your order is immediately placed on your account. The Dash Wand is Amazon's latest device. Like the Hiku, it can scan barcodes or react to your voice.

Soap, check. Cereal, check. Milk, check! Devices such as the Dash Button will order your shopping for you.

THE STORE OF THE FUTURE

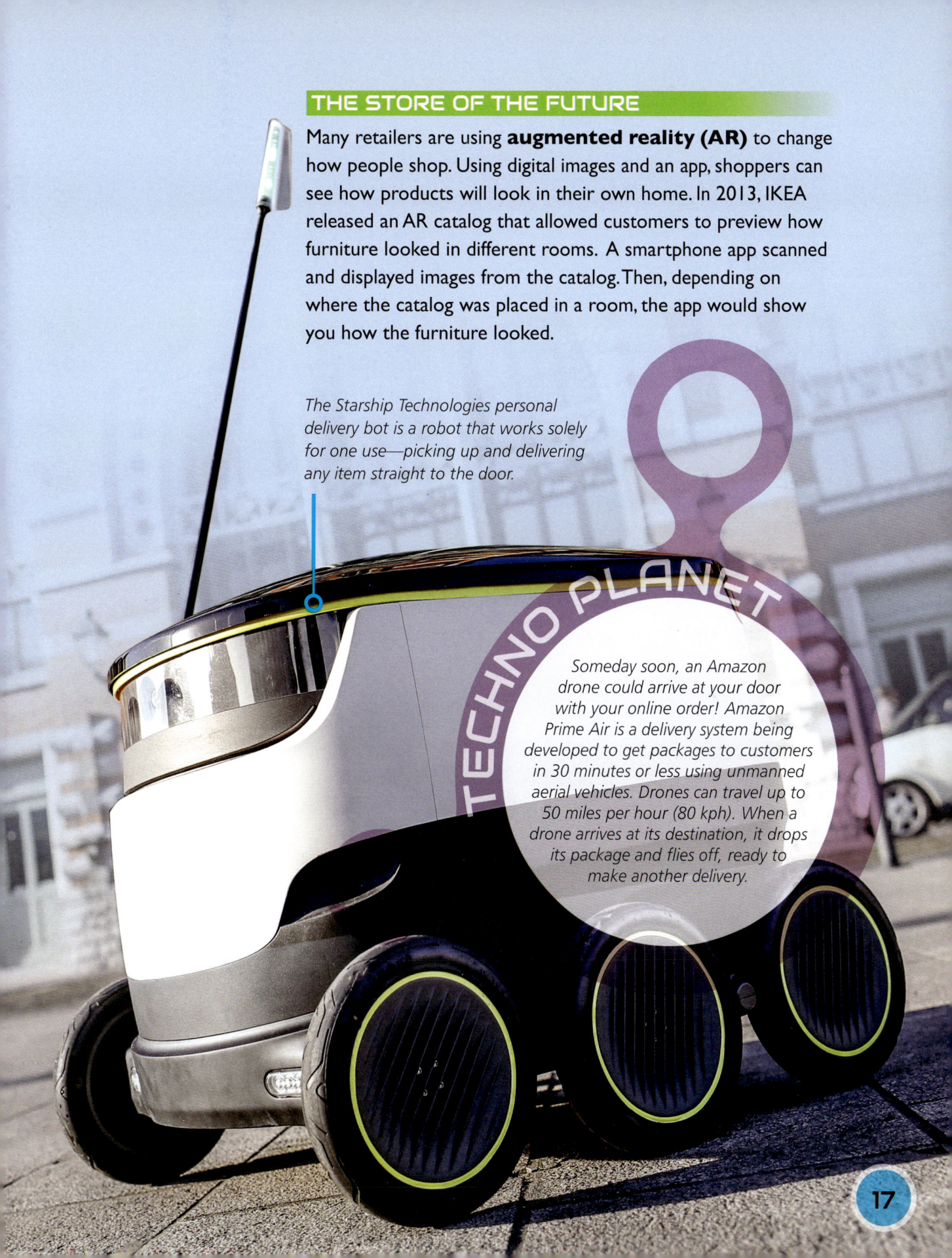

Many retailers are using **augmented reality (AR)** to change how people shop. Using digital images and an app, shoppers can see how products will look in their own home. In 2013, IKEA released an AR catalog that allowed customers to preview how furniture looked in different rooms. A smartphone app scanned and displayed images from the catalog. Then, depending on where the catalog was placed in a room, the app would show you how the furniture looked.

The Starship Technologies personal delivery bot is a robot that works solely for one use—picking up and delivering any item straight to the door.

Someday soon, an Amazon drone could arrive at your door with your online order! Amazon Prime Air is a delivery system being developed to get packages to customers in 30 minutes or less using unmanned aerial vehicles. Drones can travel up to 50 miles per hour (80 kph). When a drone arrives at its destination, it drops its package and flies off, ready to make another delivery.

SMART WEAR

From head to toe, companies are proving that clothes can be fashionable and functional. Clothing items with built-in technologies are known as wearables. Some wearables are designed to make life easier, improve safety, and even monitor signs of health and fitness. Others are used simply to showcase creativity paired with technology.

ON THE RUNWAY

People often dress in clothes that reflect how they feel. In some futuristic fashions, a person's feelings or thoughts physically become part of their outfit. In 2012, fashion designers CuteCircuit debuted the Twitter Dress, which featured more than 10,000 LED lights woven into the fabric. The dress could receive Tweets in real-time, using the hashtag #tweetthedress.

EYE TO EYE

Spectacles are stylish sunglasses released by Snap Inc., the company behind the photo- and video-sharing app Snapchat. The glasses record ten seconds of video of what the wearer is seeing, and these videos can then be wirelessly uploaded to Snapchat. A ring of lights around the camera lets people know when the glasses are recording.

The Moverio BT-200 smart glasses, produced by the Epson company, allow you to make the most of augmented reality apps and view **three-dimensional (3-D)** or **high definition (HD)** video right in front of your eyes. The product offers a variety of AR apps. One, for example, can tell you all about the stars as you look at the night sky. Another even teaches you how to play the piano!

Snap Inc.'s Spectacles are fun to wear and make sharing video almost instant.

TECHNO PLANET

POWER UP

Some fabrics have built-in solar panels that you can use to charge a smartphone! The Solar Shirt has 120 solar cells woven into the fabric that collect energy from the Sun. Loomia, a New York City smart fabrics business, is working with the clothes store Topshop. It aims to produce clothes that will measure your body temperature and even tell you if your body posture is wrong.

Project Jacquard is an innovative collaboration between Google and the clothing company Levi's. The technology allows for any fabric to work like a touch screen. **Conductive** threads are woven through the material. The threads connect to a tab that sends commands to the wearer's smartphone. Simply swiping the sleeve allows wearers to perform tasks such as skipping a song. The first product to use this technology was a jacket designed to make it safer for couriers to use their smartphones while cycling.

Fashion-forward dressers will love these state-of-the-art outfits made by CuteCircuit. They include LED lights and Tweet-receiving technology!

CUTTING-EDGE COMMUNICATION

Smartphones have revolutionized how we connect with one another. They allow us to talk, text, e-mail, and video chat from the comfort of our homes to almost anywhere on the planet in real time. New advances in software, usually made available as apps for phones, tablets, and computers, now allow us to do even more. In the future, we may even be able to control these apps using signals from our brain picked up on tiny headsets and sent wirelessly.

VIRTUAL PEOPLE

Room2Room is an augmented reality technology being developed by Microsoft. Multiple cameras capture video of a person from different angles. An image of the person is then projected into the space where another person is physically located. The two people can interact as though they were in the same room. The Room2Room system decides where to place the virtual person in the room based on where other people are seated. If a person sits on the virtual person's lap, the image shifts to a new location.

TRANSLATION TECH

The Pilot is a set of linked earpieces that translate foreign languages in real time. Each speaker wears an earpiece. As the first person talks, their words are fed through the Pilot app. The app translates the words into the language spoken by the second person. A translated version is then played in the second person's earpiece. The earpieces cancel out noises other than the conversation. The first generation Pilot app can translate five languages—English, French, Portuguese, Spanish, and Italian.

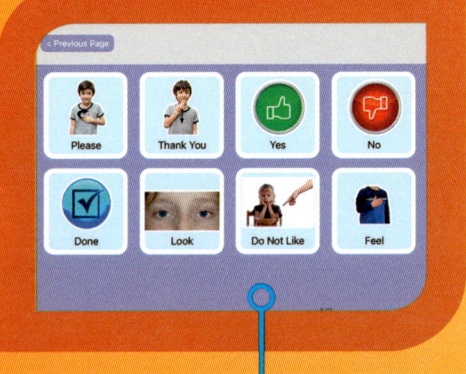

App2Talk technology could change the lives of people who cannot communicate easily. Pictures are linked to spoken words in this smart but simple communication system.

BREAKING DOWN BARRIERS

There are people who spend a lot of time at home because of health issues. Some of these people have problems communicating. Technology can help give everyone a voice. App2Talk is a tool specially designed for people who find it difficult to speak. It uses pictures to communicate a person's needs. The app can be easily used on a smartphone or tablet. Computers and tablets can also be used to create a "voice," with special text-to-speech software.

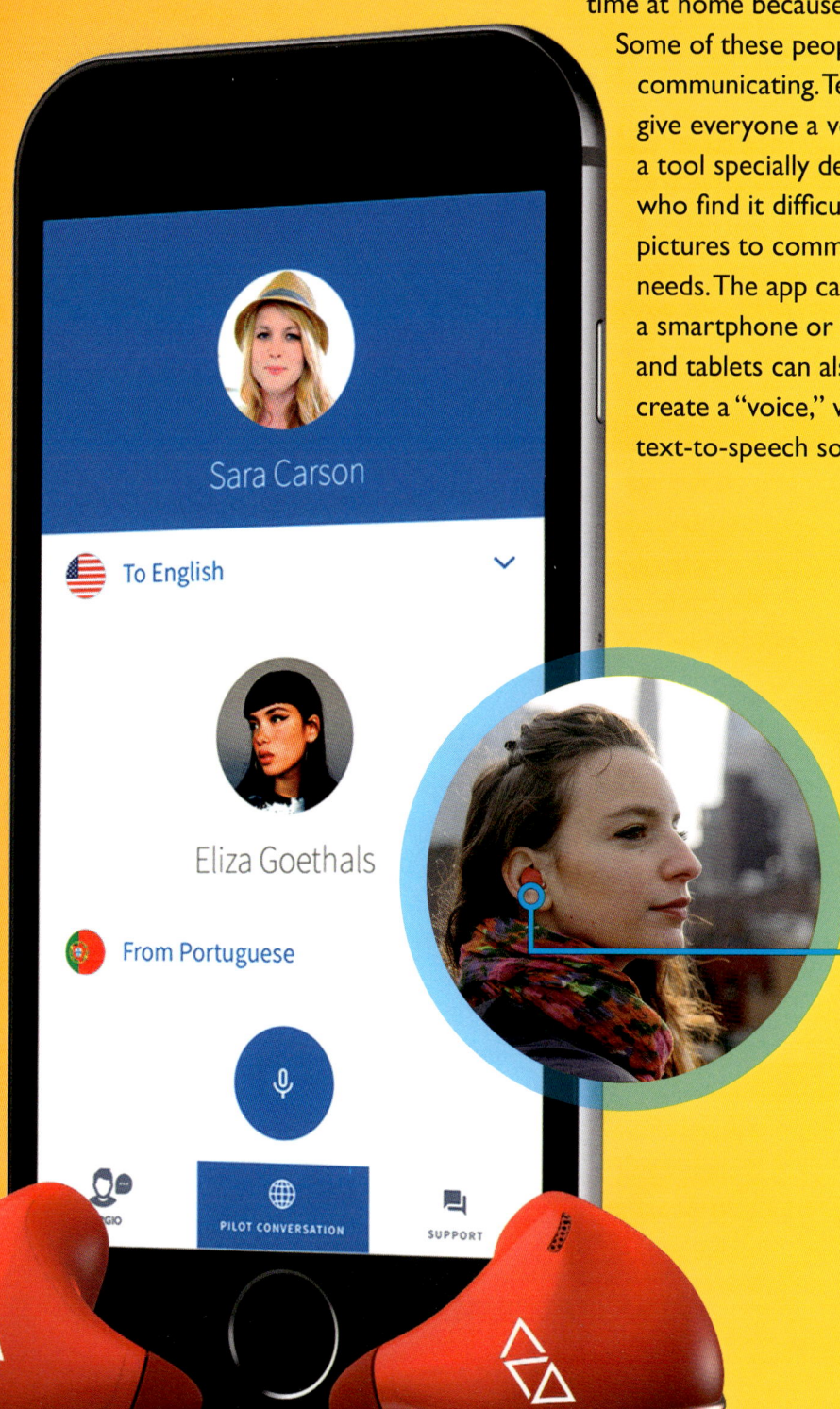

Traveling and speaking abroad could become a breeze with the Pilot. The app and smart earpiece tech could soon extend to many more languages than the five already covered.

21

ELECTRONIC ENTERTAINMENT

For decades, the entertainment industry has been changing how people experience video games, TV, movies, and music. Companies are always competing with one another to bring out new gadgets and software to create a more **immersive** entertainment experience.

LIGHTING UP THE WALLS

Lightform is a device that allows any surface to turn into a screen that images can be projected onto. First, a camera scans the room. Then, computer software creates a 3-D map that shows the different surfaces that the projector can focus an image on. This technology can be used to show a movie on the walls of a room.

MORE REAL THAN REAL

Virtual reality uses technology to trick your brain into believing you are inside a real environment, when it is actually computer-generated. This sensation is known as **telepresence.** Sensors inside a VR headset track, or follow, how you move your head. The images on the display inside the headset respond to the movement. The FOVE VR headset, developed in Japan, even responds to the wearer's eye movements.

ART AT YOUR FINGERTIPS

Google Arts & Culture is a website and app that brings together art and technology. The project has digitized thousands of works of art and created an online gallery where they can be viewed at home from your laptop or tablet. Some famous pieces are captured as a gigapixel image. A gigapixel contains more than 1 billion pixels, which are the small dots that form a picture.

Smart technology is revolutionizing the way we entertain ourselves. Using the Lightform, movie-watching will be possible almost anywhere.

These **high-resolution** images give people a close-up look at different artworks. Some paintings are so detailed you can even see the brushstrokes!

Arts & Culture also allows people to explore world-famous museums from home. To create this virtual reality experience, a special camera is rolled through a museum on a trolley. A computer uses GPS technology to build a map of the museum. Then the pictures are stitched together to create a 360-degree view of each room. The Metropolitan Museum of Art in New York City and the Royal Ontario Museum in Toronto, Canada, are two museums that can be explored through the Arts & Culture project.

Virtual reality is opening up endless possibilities in the world of entertainment and education. Imagine learning in a 3-D world! This could soon become a reality in homes, schools, and colleges.

TECHNO PLANET

In Utah, a theme park called The Void offers an added level of immersion. In a large arena, a virtual environment has been mapped over the physical space. Gamers suit up with VR headsets and connected vests, then travel through the virtual world—both physically and mentally.

BRAINWAVES

In the *Star Wars* movies, Jedi Knights have the ability to control objects with the power of their minds. What was once only possible in our imagination may one day soon be reality. Technology is now being used to learn and express human emotions and thoughts.

CATCHING WAVES

The human brain is a complex organ. It is filled with billions of cells called neurons. Connections between neurons generate low levels of electricity. Electroencephalography (EEG) is a technique used to detect and record these electric pulses. Small, flat sensors called **electrodes** are placed on a person's head. The electrodes detect the electrical pulses and send the information to a machine that shows the brain activity as wavy lines. Today, EEG technology has been embedded into brainwear, which are wearables that interact with a person's mind. Brainwear such as the Emotiv headset has built-in EEG sensors that send readings to an app. The Emotiv Insight has five EEG sensors that measure the wearer's brain activity. The data is sent to an app on that person's smartphone, computer, or tablet.

Smart technology such as the Emotiv headset could help us learn more about how our thoughts and feelings change throughout the day.

UNDERSTANDING EMOTIONS

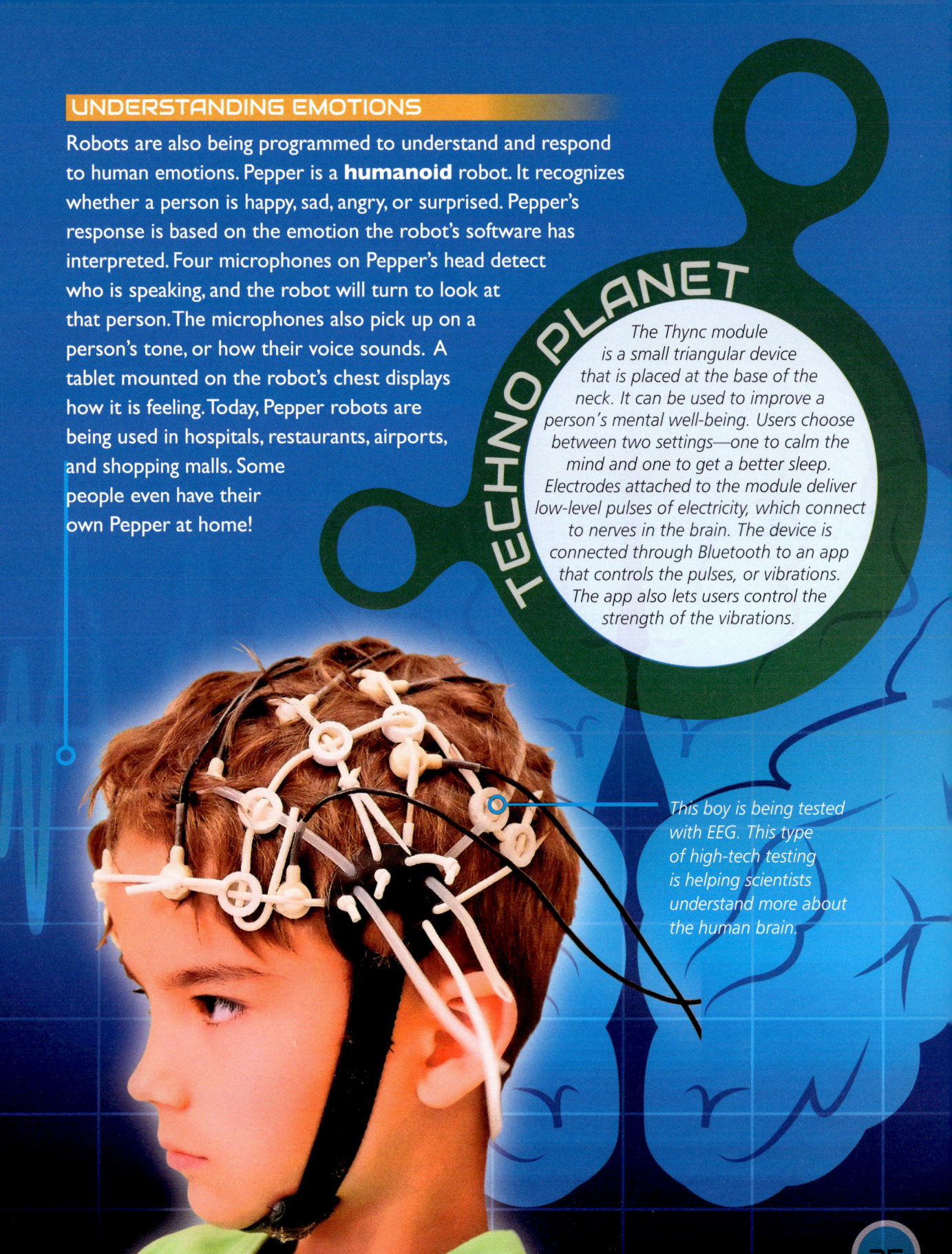

Robots are also being programmed to understand and respond to human emotions. Pepper is a **humanoid** robot. It recognizes whether a person is happy, sad, angry, or surprised. Pepper's response is based on the emotion the robot's software has interpreted. Four microphones on Pepper's head detect who is speaking, and the robot will turn to look at that person. The microphones also pick up on a person's tone, or how their voice sounds. A tablet mounted on the robot's chest displays how it is feeling. Today, Pepper robots are being used in hospitals, restaurants, airports, and shopping malls. Some people even have their own Pepper at home!

TECHNO PLANET

The Thync module is a small triangular device that is placed at the base of the neck. It can be used to improve a person's mental well-being. Users choose between two settings—one to calm the mind and one to get a better sleep. Electrodes attached to the module deliver low-level pulses of electricity, which connect to nerves in the brain. The device is connected through Bluetooth to an app that controls the pulses, or vibrations. The app also lets users control the strength of the vibrations.

This boy is being tested with EEG. This type of high-tech testing is helping scientists understand more about the human brain.

FUTURE FANTASTIC

Every day, innovators are shaping the future. They dream up and design new gizmos and gadgets that will change how we live. Here are just a few technologies that you may see in the not-too-distant future.

HOME HELP AND HEALTH

There are already simple robots, such as iRobot and Neato, which can move around the home and clean floors. However, scientists are now working on robots that will have arms and fingers that can pick things up, tidy the home, operate machines, and even serve you a drink. They will work from a touch screen or react to voice commands and even hand movements.

A toilet is just a toilet, right? Not in the future. Soon, smart toilets will use sensors to analyze what we put into them, sending information to our smartphones and even to health practitioners. This technology might even be able to tell someone if they have cancer or are pregnant.

HEADING INTO 5G

In the future, our communications systems will need to support billions of connected devices around the world. The next generation of wireless network is called 5G. This new communications system is expected to launch in the 2020s. New technologies are being explored to allow for faster connections with less **latency** and greater reliability. Millimeter waves are radio waves that are sent at a higher **frequency** than what we use now. Connection speeds with 5G will be about 1,000 times faster than what is currently available through 4G networks.

Look out for the next-generation wireless network. 5G will make sending and receiving communications even faster in the future!

BACKING UP THE BRAIN

One day we will be able to access the Internet, and all the information it contains, with the power of our minds. We will also be able to control electronic devices through a **Brain–Computer Interface (BCI)**. A BCI is a chip that is implanted inside a person's head. The chip will use electric pulses from the brain to form new connections between the brain and the chip. The smartphone will no longer be king of the castle. Imagine the possibilities!

Imagine being able to control all your electronic devices just by thinking! A BCI chip inside the brain will enable the user to do just that. Welcome to the world of high-tech living!

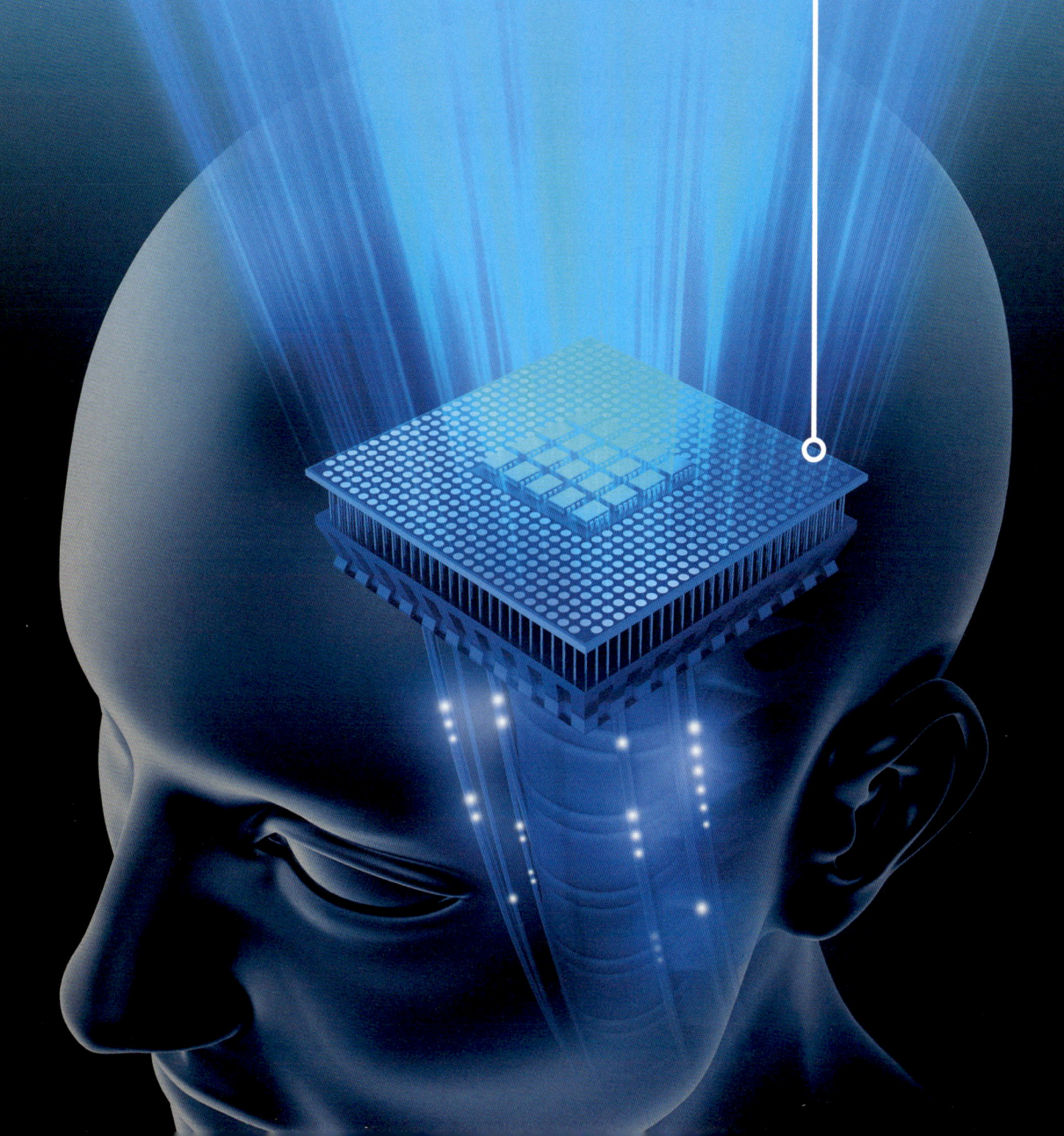

TECH TIMELINE

1700 B.C.E. The Minoan Palace at Knossos on Crete uses gold and silver faucets

1876 Alexander Graham Bell makes the first telephone call in Ontario, Canada

1892 Thomas Ahearn invents the electric oven in Ottawa, Canada

1907 The first practical, portable home vacuum cleaner is invented

1919 The first automatic toaster pops up

1931 Jacob Schick launches the electric shaver

1964 The first flat-screen TV is invented

1596 Sir John Harrington invents the flushable toilet in England

1877 The phonograph plays sound recorded on cardboard cylinders coated with wax

1902 The first modern air conditioning unit is installed

1913 The first electric refrigerators are sold to homes

1920s Crystal radio receivers find their way into living rooms

1948 The first LP records are made

28

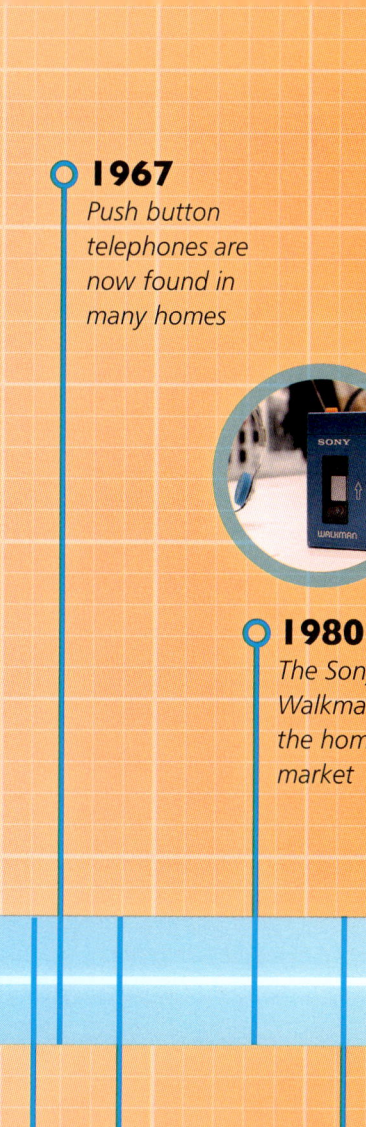

1967
Push button telephones are now found in many homes

1993
IBM releases the first smartphone, with a touch screen and programs such as a calendar and calculator

2009
Google launches its self-driving car project

1980
The Sony Walkman hits the home market

1997
Electrolux presents the first robot vacuum cleaner

2015
A drone makes the first successful delivery of a package in the United States

1965
Microwave ovens are available to buy

1970s
Compact discs (CDs) are developed

1991
British scientist Tim Berners-Lee creates the software that forms the foundation of the World Wide Web

1994
PlayStation is released in Japan

2001
Apple introduces the iPod

2006
Nintendo Wii brings the concept of control by movement into the home

29

GLOSSARY

Please note: Some **bold-faced** words are defined where they appear in the book.

analog A kind of signal that changes continually, like the sound from a loudspeaker

atomizer A machine that sprays out a fine mist

augmented reality (AR) Technology that overlays computer-generated images on the real world

autonomous Being able to function independently

Bluetooth A wireless technology used to connect devices across short distances

conductive Being able to carry energy or information

converts Changes from one form to another

digital A kind of signal that is fixed, like the time display on your cell phone

dock A device where a wireless device is placed to charge

efficient Productive

electrodes Small devices that allow electricity to flow into or out of a body

frequency The number of radio waves that pass a fixed point each second

global positioning system (GPS) A navigation system that uses satellite signals to fix locations

gyroscope A wheel mounted to spin rapidly so that its axis is free to turn in various directions

high definition (HD) Particularly clear and precise, as in a TV picture

high-resolution Particularly clear and precise, as in a photograph or other image

humanoid Appearing to resemble a human

immersive Creating a 3-D image that appears to surround the user

innovative Having and using new ideas

interface Where two or more systems meet

latency The delay in transmitting data

microchip A group of electronic circuits on a tiny piece of material

navigate To find the way

networks Two or more computers that are connected

sensors Devices that sense something, such as motion, and react to it

syncs Synchronizes with something

telepresence The feeling of being somewhere else created by virtual reality

thermostat A device that turns something on or off at a particular temperature

three-dimensional (3-D) Having or seeming to have the three dimensions of length, width, and height

touch screen A screen that displays options that can be selected by touch

virtual reality (VR) An artificial world created by a computer that a person interacts with

LEARNING MORE

BOOKS

Abell, Tracy. *All About Drones*. Focus Readers, 2017.

Anniss, Matt. *How Does WiFi Work?* Gareth Stevens, 2014.

Blakemore, Megan. *All About Smart Technology*. Focus Readers, 2017.

Editors of *TIME for Kids Magazine*. *TIME for Kids Book of WHAT: Everything Inventions*. Time, 2015.

Marsico, Katie. *Self-Driving Cars*. Scholastic, 2016.

WEBSITES

www.fi.edu/understanding-artificial-intelligence
The Franklin Institute provides a Q&A with a scientist on how machines can imitate human behavior and how this is being applied to different technologies today.

www.smithsonianmag.com/innovation/10-new-ways-use-drones-180960061
This article from the *Smithsonian* examines new and innovative ways drone technology is being used.

www.popularmechanics.com/technology/infrastructure/g89/8-ways-magnetic-levitation-could-shape-the-future
Popular Mechanics lists eight ways magnetic levitation can be applied in the future.

https://waymo.com/tech
Visit the Waymo site to learn about the ground-breaking technology behind Google's self-driving car.

INDEX

air conditioning 28
alarm clocks 9
Alexa 6
Amazon Echo 6
Amazon products 6, 16, 17
App2Talk 20, 21
apps 5, 7, 8, 10, 16, 17, 20
art galleries, virtual 22
augmented reality (AR) 17, 18, 20

Bell, Alexander Graham 28
Berners-Lee, Tim 29
Bluetooth 4
brain activity 24, 25, 27
Brain–Computer Interface (BCI) 27

clothing 18–19
communication technologies 20–21
compact discs (CDs) 29
cooking pots 10
crystal radios 28
CuteCircuit 18, 19

Dash Buttons and Wands 16
drones 17, 29

e-bikes 12
eating 5, 11
electric ovens 28
electric shavers 28

electroencephalography (EEG) 24, 25
Emotiv Insight headset 24

faucets 28
feeding pets 14
5G technologies 4, 26
flat-screen TVs 28
f.lux app 8
FOVE VR headsets 22
fridges 10–11, 28
future technologies 26–27

generations of technology 4, 26
GeniCan app 16
glasses 18
Google Arts & Culture 22–23
GPS 8, 15
grocery ordering 10, 16

HAPIfork 5
health 26
Hiku device 16
homes 5, 6–7
hoverboards 12–13
humanoid robots 25

IKEA AR catalog 17
Internet of Things (IoT) 4
invisible fences 15
iPod 29

kitchen technologies 10–11

LG InstaView refrigerator 10
Lightform 22
LP (long playing) records 28

microchipping pets 14, 15
microwave ovens 29
Moverio BT-200 glasses 18
museums, virtual 23

Nintendo Wii 29

online shopping 10, 16, 17

Passport Pet Access Smart Door 14
Pepper robot 25
Perfect Bake Pro 10
personal delivery bots 17
pet technologies 14–15
PetChatz 14
Petcube cameras 14, 15
phonographs 28
Pilot 20, 21
playing with pets 14
Project Jacquard 19
Project Nourished 11

relaxation 25
robotic vacuums 6, 7, 26, 29
Room2Room 20

scents 9, 11
security, home 7
self-driving cars 12, 29
Sensorwake alarm 9
Sleep Number 360 beds 8
sleep technologies 8, 25
SmartBowl 14
smartphones 4, 7, 8, 10, 11, 16, 17, 19, 20, 21, 27, 28
Snap Inc. Spectacles 18
Snapchat 18
Solar Shirt 19
Sony Walkman 29
Starship Technologies 17

telephones 28, 29
The Void theme park 23
Thync module 25
toasters 28
toilets 26, 28
touch screens 10, 11
translation apps 20, 21
Twitter Dress 18, 19

vacuums 6, 7, 26, 28, 29
virtual reality (VR) 11, 22–23

WalkCar 13
wearable technology 108–119
Wi-Fi 4, 16
wireless networks 4, 26
World Wide Web 29

About the Author
Kelly Spence works as a freelance author and editor for educational publishers. She holds a BA in English and Liberal Arts from Brock University, and a Certificate in Publishing from Ryerson University.

32